Ten Apples Up On Top!

D0551980

By
Dr. Seuss

writing as
Theo. LeSieg

illustrated by Roy McKie

COLLINS

I CAN READ IT ALL BY MYSELF

Beginner Books

Trademark of Random House Inc.
Authorised user HarperCollins*Publishers* Ltd

CONDITIONS OF SALE
The paperback edition of this book is sold subject to the
condition that it shall not, by way of trade or otherwise,
be lent, re-sold, hired out or otherwise circulated
without the publisher's written consent in any form of
binding or cover other than that in which it is published
and without a similar condition, including this condition
being imposed on the subsequent purchaser.

10 9

ISBN 0 00 171323 X (paperback)
ISBN 0 00 171112 1 (hardback)

© 1961, 1989 by Dr. Seuss Enterprises, L.P.
All Rights Reserved

A Beginner Book published by arrangement with
Random House Inc., New York, USA
First published in the UK 1963

Printed and bound in Hong Kong

One apple
up on top!

Two apples
up on top!

4

Look, you.

I can do it, too.

Look!

See!

I can do three!

Three . . .

Three . . .

I see.

I see.

You can do three
but I can do more.
You have three
but I have four.

Look! See, now.

I can hop

with four apples

up on top.

And I can hop
up on a tree
with four apples
up on me.

Look here, you two.

See here, you two.

I can get five

on top.

Can you?

I am so good
I will not stop.
Five!
Now six!
Now seven on top!

Seven apples
up on top!

I am
so good
they will not drop.

Five, six, seven!

Fun, fun, fun!

Seven, six, five,

four, three, two, one!

But, see!
We are as good as you.
Look! Now we
have seven, too.

And now, see here.

Eight! Eight on top!

Eight apples up!

Not one will drop.

Eight! Eight!
And we can skate.
Look now!
We can skate
with eight.

But I can do nine.
And hop!
And drink!
You can not do this,
I think.

We can! We can!

We can do it, too.

See here.

We are as good as you!

We all are very good
I think.
With nine, we all
can hop and drink.

Nine is very good.
But then . . .
Come on and we
will make it ten!

Look!

Ten

apples

up

on

top!

We are not

going to let them drop!

Look out!
Look out!
I see a mop.

I will make
the apples fall.
Get out. Get out. You!
One and all!

Come on! Come on!
Come down this hall.
We must not let
our apples fall!

Out of our way!
We can not stop.
We can not let
our apples drop.

This is not good.
What will we do?
They want to get
our apples, too.

They will get them
if we let them.
Come! We can not
let them get them.

Look out!

The mop!

The mop!

The mop!

You can not stop
our apple fun.
Our apples will not drop.
Not one!

Come on! Come on!
Come one! Come all!
We have to make
the apples fall.

They must not get
our apples down.
Come on! Come on!
Get out of town!

Apples!

Apples up on top!

All of this

must stop

STOP

STOP!

Now all our fun
is going to stop!
Our apples all
are going to drop.

Look!
Ten apples
on us all!

What fun!
We will not
let them fall.

Learning to read is fun with Beginner Books

I CAN READ IT ALL BY MYSELF

Beginner Books

FIRST get started with:

Ten Apples Up On Top
Dr. Seuss

Go Dog Go
P D Eastman

Put Me in the Zoo
Robert LopShire

THEN gain confidence with:

Dr. Seuss's ABC*
Dr. Seuss

Fox in Sox*
Dr. Seuss

Green Eggs and Ham*
Dr. Seuss

Hop on Pop*
Dr. Seuss

I Can Read With My Eyes Shut
Dr. Seuss

I Wish That I Had Duck Feet
Dr. Seuss

One Fish, Two Fish*
Dr. Seuss

Oh, the Thinks You Can Think!
Dr. Seuss

Please Try to Remember the First of Octember
Dr. Seuss

Wacky Wednesday
Dr. Seuss

Are You My Mother?
P D Eastman

Because a Little Bug Went Ka-choo!
Rosetta Stone

Best Nest
P D Eastman

Come Over to My House
Theo. LeSieg

The Digging-est Dog
Al Perkins

I Am Not Going to Get Up Today!
Theo. LeSieg

It's Not Easy Being a Bunny!
Marilyn Sadler

I Want to Be Somebody New
Robert LopShire

Maybe You Should Fly a Jet!
Theo. LeSieg

Robert the Rose Horse
Joan Heilbroner

The Very Bad Bunny
Joan Heilbroner

THEN take off with:

The Cat in the Hat*
Dr. Seuss

The Cat in the Hat Comes Back*
Dr. Seuss

Oh Say Can You Say?
Dr. Seuss

My Book About Me
Dr. Seuss

A Big Ball of String
Marion Holland

Chitty Chitty Bang Bang!
Ian Fleming

A Fish Out of Water
Helen Palmer

A Fly Went By
Mike McClintock

The King, the Mice and the Cheese
N & E Gurney

Sam and the Firefly
P D Eastman

BERENSTAIN BEAR BOOKS
By Stan & Jan Berenstain

The Bear Detectives

The Bear Scouts

The Bears' Christmas

The Bears' Holiday

The Bears' Picnic

The Berenstain Bears and the Missing Dinosaur Bones

The Big Honey Hunt

The Bike Lesson

THEN you won't quite be ready to go to college. But you'll be well on your way!

*From the Dr. Seuss Classic Collection